ROCK WHAT YA GOT

By Samantha Berger

Illustrated by Kerascoët

L B

Little, Brown and Company
New York Boston

For my mother, Eileen Kitzis Berger,
who gave me a lotta what I got to rock. — S.B.

Dear Reader,
This book is about loving yourself, finding the best
parts of what makes you YOU, and ROCKING
them to the utmost—without judgment on reconstruction,
alteration, transformation, or any other changes one
makes to one's self or one's life. You do you, and you
be true, and whatever ya got – ROCK! ❤ *S. B.*

ABOUT THE BOOK The art for this book was created using watercolor and colored pencils on Arches paper. This book was edited by Andrea Spooner and designed by Nicole Brown with art direction by David Caplan. The production was supervised by Virginia Lawther, and the production editor was Annie McDonnell. The text was set in Alice, and the display type is handlettered.

Once upon a

blank piece of paper,

where anything could happen...

an artist picked up a
pencil and started to draw.

She drew a face, and a body, and two feet.
Then she gave her drawing a name.

Viva

The artist sighed deeply.
Something wasn't quite right.
So she decided to erase her
drawing and start again.

But before she could,
Viva grabbed the pencil
and tried to stop her.

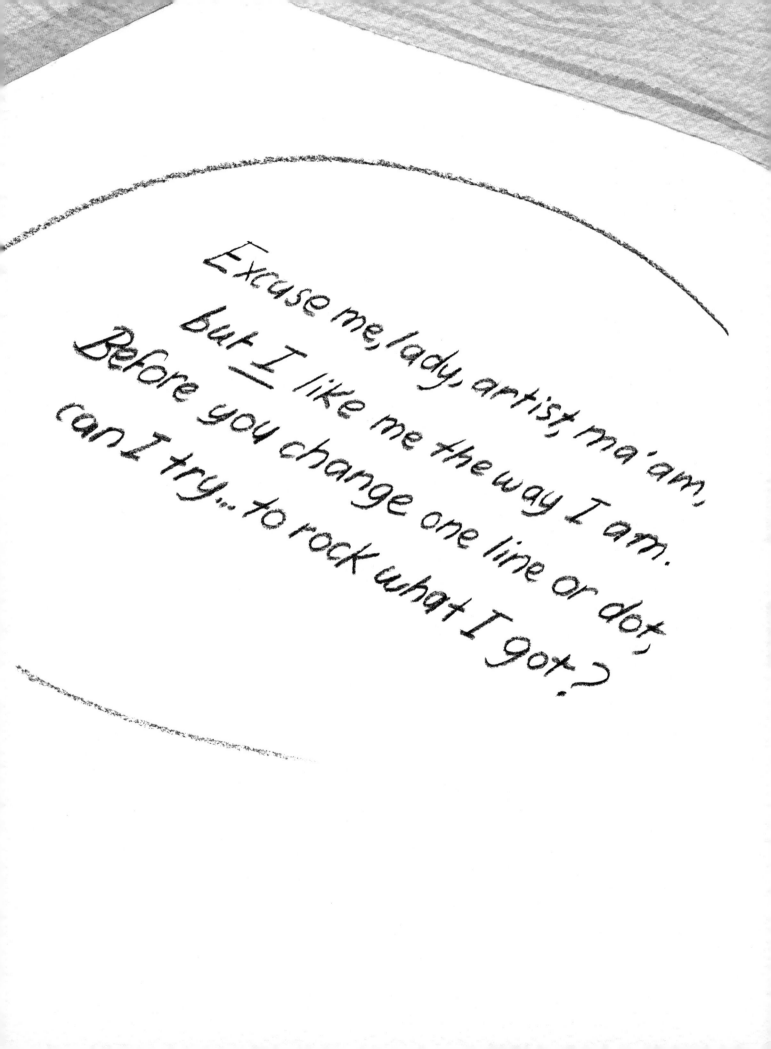

Excuse me, lady, artist, ma'am,
but I like me the way I am.
Before you change one line or dot,
can I try... to rock what I got?

The artist thought.
But decided not.
What exactly didn't she like?

A-HA!

It was the
HAIR!

Maybe if the hair was different,
this drawing could work.

So she turned the page...

and tried
changing the hair.

But after all the trying,
it was still Viva on the page.
And she had more to say.

Rock what ya got
and rock it a lot,

Look at what IS,
not what is NOT!

The artist thought.
But decided not.
What exactly didn't she like?

A-HA!

It was the
BODY!

Maybe if the body was different,
this drawing could work.

So she turned the page...

and tried changing the body.

But after all the trying,
it was still Viva on the page.
And she still had something to say.

Everyone has their own special thing—
find what is yours,
and bring what you bring....

Find your own voice
and sing how you sing,
Find your own OOMPH!
Find your own ZING!

The artist thought.
But decided not.
What exactly didn't she like?

A-HA!

It was the

BACKGROUND!

Maybe if the background was different,
this drawing could work.

So she turned the page...

and tried changing the entire background.
She drew an enchanted forest with a
dazzling palace,

wild unicorns, and
a handsome prince,
in full color.

But after *all that,* it was still Viva on the page.
And she was still saying that same familiar thing.

Rock what ya got and rock it a lot.
Don't let anyone say what you're NOT.

The artist thought.
*Was there a chance
that she forgot?*

There was.

Because she was the one
who had written it—a long time ago,
when she was just about Viva's age.

The artist made herself a promise
never to forget again.

And she decided Viva was
perfect just the way she was,
rocking exactly what she had.

Then together,
they turned the page...

where
anything
could happen.